REVENGE OF THE MUMMY

Mike,

Hope you enjoy
the book!

Mrs. Masterson

Look for these books in the
Clue™ series:

REVENGE OF THE MUMMY

Book created by A. E. Parker

Written by Marie Jacks

Based on characters from the Parker Brothers® game

A Creative Media Applications Production

SCHOLASTIC INC.
New York Toronto London Auckland Sydney

Special thanks to: Susan Nash, Laura Millhollin, Maureen Taxter, Jean Feiwel, Ellie Berger, Greg Holch, Dona Smith, Nancy Smith, John Simko, David Tommasino, Jennifer Presant, and Elizabeth Parisi

ISBN 0-590-62376-1

Copyright © 1996 by Waddingtons Games, a division of Hasbro UK Limited. All rights reserved. Published by Scholastic Inc. by arrangement with Parker Brothers, a division of Tonka Corporation. CLUE® is a registered trademark of Waddingtons Games for its detective game equipment.

12 11 10 9 8 7 6 5 4   7 8 9/9 0/0

Printed in the U.S.A.   40

First Scholastic printing, June 1996

To all our readers

Contents

REVENGE OF THE MUMMY

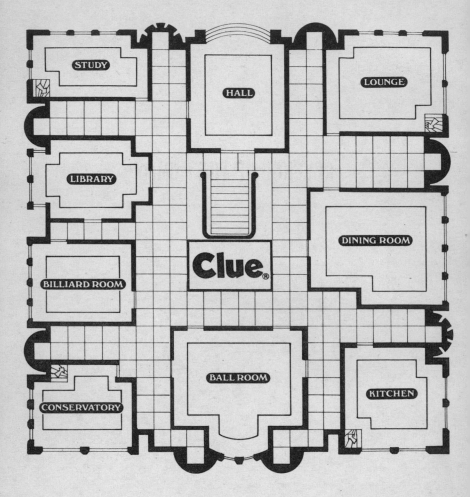

Allow Me to Introduce Myself . . .

WELCOME!

My name is Reginald Boddy. I shall be your host for another visit to my mansion.

I don't know if you know this, but the mansion is a historical landmark. But not because a treaty was signed on the premises or because a famous writer or inventor once lived here. The mansion is legendary because it's the site of so many crimes.

For example, the last time my guests visited, I was left for dead in the Dining Room, murdered by a wild Professor Plum who thought himself under the spell of a haunted gargoyle. Fortunately, in his frenzy, he did me little physical harm. My feelings are still hurt by the fact that one of my guests would attempt to do me in, even though it happens so often.

Perhaps I'm the crazy one, since I've invited these same guests back for another visit to my mansion.

In a few moments I shall be joining them in the Library. (My guests are so famous that a dozen

1

books have already been written about them.) They're the nicest people in the world — when they're not after my valuable possessions or each other. And, since you've chosen to join us here at the mansion, would you please help me keep track of them?

There are six guests, including my maid, Mrs. White. (I will never be a suspect in any wrongdoing. You have my word on this, as a gentleman.) The six guests you need to keep track of are:

Mr. Green: A businessman whose greed has gotten the best of him on several occasions. Once he helped an old lady across a busy street, then charged her for the favor.

Colonel Mustard: He believes even the slightest disagreement is best settled by fighting a duel. Rumor has it that he challenged a friend to match pistols at dawn after the friend took the last cookie in the cookie jar.

Mrs. Peacock: Although she is a most refined lady who always demonstrates proper manners, there is no truth to the gossip that she was born wearing white gloves.

Professor Plum: A man with many advanced degrees, though what he displays most is an advanced degree of forgetfulness. Plum's explanation is that after many years of giving countless students the benefit of his knowledge, he has precious little left for himself.

Miss Scarlet: The woman has more than a hint of mystery about her. The greatest mystery is why I keep inviting her back. Perhaps the answer lies in her spellbinding beauty.

Mrs. White: She has been in my service for many years and, sadly, has committed her share of crimes. Friends suggest that I should get rid of Mrs. White. I would, but I'm afraid that if I tried, she would get rid of me first.

There. A more arresting group of guests you won't find anywhere. And if they don't behave themselves this time, I'll have them all arrested!

At the end of each chapter a list of rooms, suspects, and weapons is provided so that you may keep track of events at the mansion.

Well, it's time to get started. My advice is to watch your step — and your back — and keep your wits about you.

Our first adventure is about to begin in the Library.

1.
The Lion Ring

COLONEL MUSTARD RUSHED INTO THE Library, where the other guests were relaxing.

"Quick!" he shouted. "Come and see Mr. Boddy's latest trophy."

"Is it a bowling trophy?" asked Professor Plum.

"It's not that kind of trophy," said Colonel Mustard. "Boddy's trophy is a wild game prize."

"A wild game prize?" asked Mr. Green. "For playing a wild game of crazy eights?"

"No, no," said Colonel Mustard.

"A blue ribbon for winning at charades?" asked Mrs. Peacock.

"No, no, no!" Colonel Mustard shouted.

"Calm down, sir," said Mrs. Peacock. "It's bad manners to shout."

"You're right," replied the colonel, "but I can't help being excited. Boddy has bagged himself a lion!"

"Mr. Boddy has a lion in a bag?" asked Mrs. White, entering from the Hall.

"I hope it's not a paper bag," said Professor Plum. "A lion could claw its way out of a paper bag — and then we'd all have to run for our lives!"

"You people are impossible!" insisted Colonel Mustard. He pulled out the Lead Pipe and threatened the others.

"Colonel, you'd best back off, or I'll knock you silly with this Candlestick," said a male guest.

"You tell him," urged Professor Plum, pulling out the Knife.

"Gentlemen, stop this improper behavior this instant," ordered the female guest with the Wrench.

"Then tell us, Colonel, what exactly *are* you talking about?" asked Mr. Green.

"Mr. Boddy just returned from a safari in Africa," explained Colonel Mustard. "While there, he captured a lion and brought it home as a trophy."

"You mean that a lion won a trophy?" asked a very confused Professor Plum.

"I know that Mr. Boddy has some rather exotic pets," observed Miss Scarlet. "Is this lion being added to the menagerie?"

"I wouldn't doubt it," said Colonel Mustard.

"I hope that Mr. Boddy has a cage strong enough to hold the beast," said Professor Plum.

"Don't worry. If there's a beast loose in the mansion, I'll capture it with this," said the female guest with the Rope.

"Or I can simply finish it off with this," replied Miss Scarlet, pulling the Revolver from her purse.

"Ladies, please settle down! Mr. Boddy told me that it's not a *live* lion," said Colonel Mustard.

"It's dead?" whispered Professor Plum. "Why, that's terrible."

"Perhaps Mrs. White will serve it for dinner," joked Mr. Green. "A lion would make a tasty *mane* course!"

Colonel Mustard shot both of the men a silencing glare. "Are you interested in viewing Mr. Boddy's lion?"

"You want to take me away from my book to see a dead beast?" asked Mr. Green, putting down *How to Double Your Money by Breakfast*, which he was reading by the glow of the Candlestick.

"Mr. Boddy swears that the lion is of great interest," reported Colonel Mustard.

"You mean it's worth money?" asked Miss Scarlet.

"I'm certain that Mr. Boddy will explain," said Colonel Mustard, leading the others from the Library to the Conservatory.

There, Mr. Boddy was standing proudly before a table with a tiny box on top of it.

"Where's the great lion that Colonel Mustard promised us?" asked Miss Scarlet.

"It's right in here," said Mr. Boddy, pointing to the box.

"There's a lion in that little thing?" asked Professor Plum with a laugh, putting away his weapon. "You must be *lion* to us."

"No, it's true," Mr. Boddy assured his guests.

"Mr. Boddy, I demand that you tell us what's going on," said Colonel Mustard. "I thought you hunted down the king of the jungle."

"From the looks of that tiny box, it looks like Boddy captured the king of the bungle," snickered Mrs. White.

"If I took the lion's share of that little box, there would be nothing left," added Mrs. Peacock.

Mr. Boddy was not bothered by his guests' remarks. "Actually, the object inside this box is quite valuable," he said.

"How exactly did you get an entire lion inside that small container?" asked Professor Plum, scratching his head. "Did you freeze-dry it?"

Boddy laughed. "Here," he said, "let me show you."

Boddy opened the box and took out a gold ring with a small, jeweled lion mounted on it. "Here's my new lion," he said proudly.

"Ah," said Mrs. Peacock. "Jewelry!"

"Here, kitty, kitty," said Miss Scarlet.

"That small ring is valuable?" asked a skeptical Mr. Green.

"It was made more than a thousand years ago for one of the great kings of Africa," Mr. Boddy informed his guests. "I had it appraised by an expert at the museum who reports that it's worth four million dollars."

"Four million? Roar!" said Mr. Green.

"Adding this lion to my collection shall increase my *pride*," boasted Boddy. "I'll be lionized from coast to coast."

"Well, I'd like my lion's share of four million dollars," Mrs. White whispered to herself.

"I'd like to sink my teeth into that money," mumbled Professor Plum.

"I must get my paws on that lion," Colonel Mustard told himself.

"Four million dollars has a nice *ring* to it," said Miss Scarlet.

"I suspect that each of you is already scheming to steal my priceless ring," observed Mr. Boddy. "But that will be quite impossible."

"And why is that?" asked Professor Plum.

"I'm locking it in my safe in the Study," said Mr. Boddy.

Several minutes later . . .

Several minutes later, having returned the lion ring to the tiny box, Mr. Boddy took it into the Study.

He was about to open his safe when a guest surprised him. "Give me that lion ring," the guest insisted. To make his point, the guest threatened Mr. Boddy with the Knife.

"May we discuss this as civilized people?" asked Mr. Boddy.

"Not as long as you have the ring," replied the

guest. "Give it to me now before *you* end up in little pieces in that box!"

Having no choice, Boddy handed over the priceless jeweled ring.

The thief escaped from the room through the secret passageway connecting it with the room at the opposite corner of the mansion.

There he emerged and was hit over the head with the Wrench.

"That should teach you not to use secret passages," the attacker said as she took the jeweled ring. "The only ring you'll have now is the ringing in your ears!"

The thief escaped next door into the room where meals were served.

"Mrs. White," said a male guest, sitting there with his back to the door, "is my snack ready? I'm as hungry as a lion."

"Not quite," said the thief, disguising her voice. Without another word, she knocked out the male guest and traded her weapon for his.

Fleeing first to the Lounge and then to the Hall, she was about to hide the jeweled lion ring there when she was attacked by the guest with the Candlestick. The thief crumpled to the floor.

The guest with the Candlestick exchanged weapons with the fallen guest and stole the ring himself. Avoiding the room where he first learned about the lion ring, he went into the Billiard Room, planning to climb out the window. But instead, he was yanked back into the room by the guest with the Rope.

"Since you're tied up," the guest said, "I'll take a few things off your hands."

The guest made off with both the ring and his weapon.

The guest with the ring rushed into the room diagonally across from the Lounge.

"At last, a place to slip this priceless ring on my finger," she said.

"Not so fast," said the guest with the Revolver.

"What do you want?" the female guest asked.

"Give me that lion or you'll be dead meat," the guest with the Revolver threatened, making a grab for the ring.

But the guest with the ring was quicker and knocked out the guest holding the Revolver. Then the guest let go a mighty victory roar.

WHO STOLE THE LION RING?

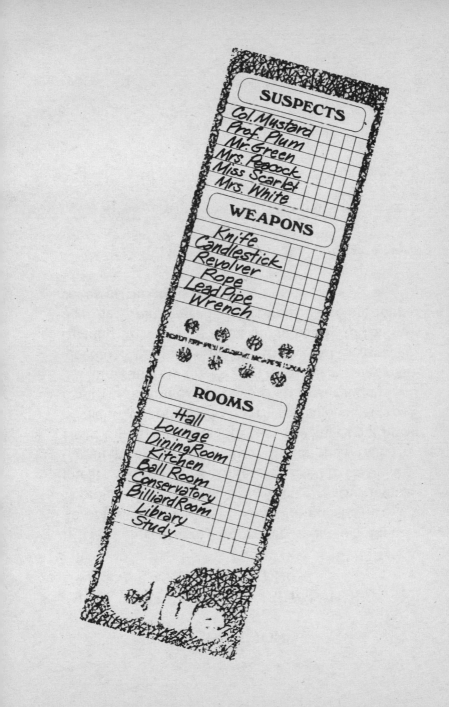

SOLUTION

MRS. WHITE in the CONSERVATORY with the LEAD PIPE

The reference to "improper behavior" identi- fies Mrs. Peacock as the female guest with the Wrench. This leaves Mrs. White as the female guest with the Rope, which she used to tie up Mr. Green in the Billiard Room. She, in turn, took the Lead Pipe, which she later used to knock out Miss Scarlet. It happened in the room diagonally across from the Lounge, which is the Conservatory.

Unfortunately for Mrs. White, her victory roar alerted Mr. Boddy to the theft. But instead of turning Mrs. White over immediately to the po- lice, he "volunteered" her to clean the big feline cages at the local zoo.

2.
Full of Hot Air

STANDING ON THE MANSION LAWN, MR. Boddy lowered a checkered flag. "Go!" he shouted.

The great hot-air balloon race was underway.

The guests had been hesitant to climb aboard individual hot-air balloons and sail across the sky — until Mr. Boddy told them that the winner would receive $25,000.

Each guest was given lessons by an expert balloonist and then outfitted with the latest safety gear. Still, some of the guests were nervous.

"If man had been meant to fly, he would've been born with wings," said Colonel Mustard.

"You're so full of hot air!" replied Mrs. White.

Fortunately, the day of the race was perfect for ballooning. The sky was clear and the wind was calm and even.

After climbing into the baskets suspended below the great balloons, each guest went through a safety check. When this was completed, they signaled Mr. Boddy that they were ready.

To avoid an argument, Mr. Boddy ordered the guests to begin the race in alphabetical order.

Mr. Green took off first. Painted on the side of his gigantic, green balloon was an enormous dollar sign.

"It never hurts to advertise," Mr. Green shouted to his fellow balloonists.

He was followed by Colonel Mustard in a yellow balloon. "It looks like the world's biggest grapefruit," joked Professor Plum.

On the side of his balloon, Colonel Mustard had painted two dueling pistols. "Maybe the pistols will go off and knock him out of the race," said Miss Scarlet.

Starting in third place was Mrs. Peacock in a blue balloon. She had printed the rules of polite ballooning on the side of her craft.

Behind her was Professor Plum in a purple balloon. He had planned to paint his self-portrait six stories high on his balloon, but unfortunately, he forgot his paints.

Miss Scarlet was next in a red balloon. On the side of her balloon she had stenciled her portrait and her phone number, in case she passed over any available billionaires.

Mrs. White brought up the rear. On her white balloon, she had written I DON'T CLEAN BALLOONS! in bold letters.

After a few minutes of maneuvering their balloons to the proper altitude, the guests began to pit their racing skills against one another.

To his dismay, Colonel Mustard watched as the female guest directly behind him pulled even.

"Lovely day for flying," she called out.

"Yes, isn't it?" he called back.

"Sorry that I can't stay around and chat," she added, "but I'm going to win the twenty-five thousand dollars."

"You're sure?" he asked.

"Quite sure," she replied. "Especially with you as my competition."

"This should slow you down," he said, lobbing the Lead Pipe into her basket.

Weighted down, the female guest's balloon dropped to the end of the line. "Colonel, that wasn't fair!" she complained.

"All is fair in war and ballooning," he replied.

Frustrated at being toward the back of the pack, the guest in the red balloon took the Knife and sent it spinning toward the leading balloon. "Good throw!" she congratulated herself.

The Knife sliced a hole in the green balloon, which slowly dropped out of contention.

"This should reduce your dollar sign to a few cents," the guest who had thrown the Knife called out.

The guest in the green balloon shook his fist at the guest who had thrown the Knife. "I'll get you, you red baroness!" he threatened.

The guest in the purple balloon realized that

now was his chance to move ahead. He threw the heavy Wrench overboard, which allowed his balloon to speed ahead and into the lead.

"I'm lighter than air," he proclaimed.

"In your head," mocked one of the other guests.

Ignoring the insult, the new leader added, "See you at the finish line!"

The guests maintained positions for a few moments. Professor Plum slowed down when a passing pigeon decided to rest in his balloon. But after coaxing the bird back in the air, the professor soon picked up speed.

"Not so fast," Mrs. White told the guest two balloons in front of her.

"Try and stop me!" the guest called back.

Mrs. White took out the Rope and lassoed the balloon.

"I don't mean to be a drag," she said, "but allow me to show you your proper place in line." Yanking hard she pulled the other balloon until it sailed behind hers.

As the remaining balloons approached the finish, the competition grew more intense.

"What I need is some more hot air," said the balloonist now in second place. She took out the second weapon she had brought along, which was the Candlestick. Quickly, she lit a candle and positioned it under the opening to the hot-air sac. Soon, additional hot air was raising from the flame into the sac.

"Come on," she said, moving the ropes that controlled the balloon. "Let's go!"

With a boost from the Candlestick, her balloon gained altitude and passed over the leader. In first place, she waved below to her competition. "See you later, slowpokes!" she called. "The twenty-five thousand dollars is as good as mine!"

Trailing badly, a furious Mrs. Peacock aimed the Revolver at the balloon from which the Wrench had been dropped.

"I'll teach you some manners," she said, squeezing the trigger.

But a sudden gust of wind spoiled her aim and the bullet knocked out the lead balloon instead.

"Well, *you* needed to learn some manners, too," said Mrs. Peacock.

"I must win that money," insisted the guest now in third place.

Working expertly, this guest maneuvered the balloon ahead of the balloon in front and crossed the finish line.

WHO WON THE BALLOON RACE?

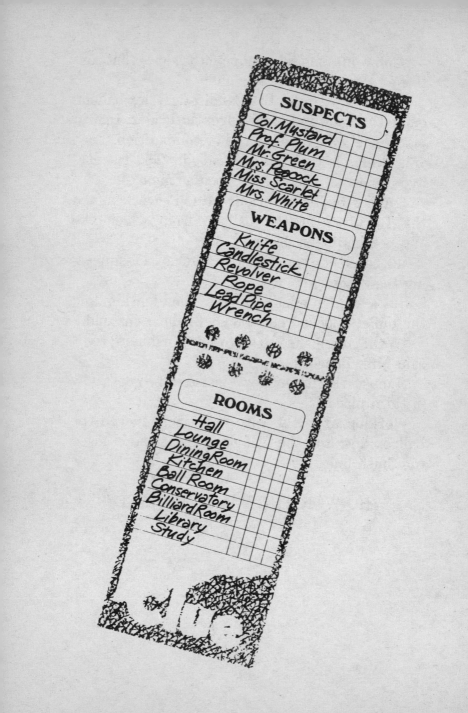

SOLUTION

COLONEL MUSTARD

Although the guests changed positions through-out the race, Colonel Mustard had been in third place since Mrs. White lassoed his balloon and pulled it directly behind hers.

His balloon was going so fast, though, that he was unable to stop it. He had to spend the $25,000 to pay for the rescue squad that pulled him out of the sky.

3.
Urge to Earn an Urn

IN THE DINING ROOM, MRS. PEACOCK was helping Mrs. White arrange some freshly cut flowers in a clay vase when Mr. Boddy came rushing into the room.

"Good gosh, ladies!" he shouted.

"You like the arrangement?" asked a hopeful Mrs. White.

"It's a classic arrangement," said Mrs. Peacock. "See how the tall stems are artfully arranged in the back. A little — but not too little — fern is added to the sides to give just a hint of — "

"What on earth do you think you're doing?" interrupted Mr. Boddy.

"First lower your voice," insisted Mrs. Peacock. "It's rude to shout at other people, and especially at me."

"Forgive me, madam," said a humbled Mr. Boddy. "But what are you doing?"

"I'm showing your maid the proper way to display flowers," said Mrs. Peacock.

"But you can't!" said Mr. Boddy.

"Sir, let me tell you that I studied floral arrangement at the world-famous Sweet William Buttercup School. I graduated first in my class," said Mrs. Peacock. "I know precisely what I'm doing."

"No surprise that her favorite flower is the *prim*rose," added Mrs. White.

"Mrs. Peacock, I'm not questioning your knowledge and skill at floral arrangements," said Mr. Boddy.

"Then what has you so hot under the collar?" she asked.

"You can't do it in *that*," he said, pointing to the vase.

"Why not?" said Mrs. White. "I found the dusty old thing in the basement. By the looks of it, you haven't used it in years. I'm simply putting it to good use."

"Have you already poured water into it?" asked Mr. Boddy.

"No, not yet," reported Mrs. White.

"Mr. Boddy, you're showing your ignorance about floral arrangements," said Mrs. Peacock. "Anyone can tell you that first you arrange the flowers, then you add the water."

"Thank goodness," said Mr. Boddy, wiping his brow.

"Mr. Boddy, you're acting very strangely. What is the matter?" asked Mrs. Peacock.

"That vase is worth five hundred sixty-five thousand dollars," he explained.

Mrs. White started to laugh — until Mr. Boddy stopped her with an icy stare.

"This old thing is worth a small fortune?" she asked.

He nodded. "I was storing it in what I thought was a safe place in the basement."

"It looks like you picked it up at a flea market," said Mrs. Peacock.

"On the contrary, I brought it home from my last trip to Greece," said Mr. Boddy. "It dates back five thousand years. It's an ancient Greek urn."

"A relic?" asked Mrs. White.

"Indeed," said Mr. Boddy. "Dozens of museums around the world would love to add it to their collections."

"Well, using it for the flowers was Mrs. White's idea," said Mrs. Peacock.

"Thanks a lot!" sighed Mrs. White. "But you, Mrs. Peacock, should have known better."

"Don't drag me into this! I never approved of this vase or urn or whatever you wish to call it."

"What's not to like?" asked a perplexed Mr. Boddy.

"It's rude!" proclaimed Mrs. Peacock.

"Rude? There's nothing rude about it. This urn is a masterpiece of antique art," explained Mr. Boddy.

"I beg to differ!" said Mrs. Peacock.

"I'm surprised that a woman of your refinement

would object to this wonderful example of classic art," said Mr. Boddy.

Barely able to look, Mrs. Peacock pointed to the nearly naked figures painted on the sides. "Art? You call this art? Talk about indecent! Someone should paint some clothes on those people!" she insisted.

Ignoring her, an angry Mr. Boddy removed the flowers and threw them to the floor.

"Hey, I paid for those flowers out of my own money!" protested Mrs. White.

"Would you rather pay to replace the urn?" asked Mr. Boddy.

"Sir, you're acting outrageously," said Mrs. Peacock.

Hearing the commotion, the other guests entered the Dining Room.

"What's all the bother?" asked Professor Plum.

"I just discovered that my priceless Greek urn was about to become a flower pot," said Mr. Boddy.

"Someone put a fern in an urn?" asked Professor Plum.

"When you say 'priceless,' what exact amount are you alluding to?" asked a curious Mr. Green.

"Let's just say it's worth a great deal of money," replied Mr. Boddy, taking the urn in his arms.

"So it's very valuable?" asked Miss Scarlet.

"Quite," Mr. Boddy assured her.

"Come on and tell us," challenged Colonel Mustard. "Are we talking a few thousand, a hundred thousand, or more than a million?"

"I've already said enough," said Mr. Boddy.

"You're quite stern about that urn," replied Mrs. Peacock.

"I guess one could earn a lot with that urn," said Mr. Green.

"I burn to get my arms on that urn," Miss Scarlet said to herself.

"I need to learn how to best steal the urn," murmured Mrs. White.

"I think it's my turn to have the urn," whispered Colonel Mustard.

"I should know better than to keep something like this here in the mansion," Mr. Boddy said. "I'm going into the Study to call my security company. First thing tomorrow, an armed guard will come and get the urn."

"But when will the urn return?" asked Professor Plum.

"When the leaves turn to auburn," said Mr. Boddy.

"But we'll be gone by then," observed Mr. Green.

"Exactly," said Mr. Boddy.

"Don't you think you're showing a bit too much concern about an urn?" asked Miss Scarlet.

"Why don't all of you go outside and work on your sunburn?" said Mr. Boddy.

With that, Mr. Boddy took the Greek urn into the Study.

Several minutes later . . .

Several minutes later, a male guest holding the Revolver entered the Study.

"Give me that urn," he told Mr. Boddy, "or I'll shatter it with a bullet."

"If you do that, no one will enjoy its beauty," reasoned Mr. Boddy.

"The only person I want to enjoy it is me!" said the guest.

"So you'd destroy a priceless relic if I refuse to give it up?" asked Mr. Boddy.

"Yes," said the guest.

Having no choice, Mr. Boddy handed over the urn.

The thief went into the Hall, where he was attacked by a female guest with the Candlestick.

"So much for your urge for the urn, Colonel," she told him.

She took the urn into the Dining Room. There, she stopped short, seeing another female picking up the flowers from the floor.

"Pardon me," said the thief, hiding the urn behind her back. "I thought the room was empty."

"Of course it's left to me to clean up any mess," said the person collecting the ruined flowers.

"These were such lovely blossoms. They were so fragrant. Would you like to smell their bouquet?"

The thief, not to draw attention to herself, agreed, but when she leaned forward, the other person knocked her out with the Lead Pipe and stole the urn.

"Some people will never learn what others will do to get the urn," the guest laughed as she left the room.

She thought of hiding the urn in the Kitchen, but the other guests would easily find it there, so she tried the Ball Room.

There, she couldn't get the light to work, so she moved to the Billiard Room.

But there, too, she couldn't find a place to hide the urn. Worried about finding a hiding place, she next tried the Library.

To her dismay, she saw another guest pulling a book down from a shelf.

"What are you reading?" she asked innocently.

"How to Marry a Millionaire When You're Already One Yourself," the guest said.

"Well, I'll leave you to your reading," she said, turning for the door.

But when she did, the guest attacked her with the Wrench and stole the urn.

He rushed through the Hall, where he considered hiding the urn in the grandfather clock. "I'll return for the urn when the clock turns three," he told himself.

26

But as he was about to, he heard someone coming down the stairs, so he strolled into the Lounge.

There, to his surprise, he was confronted by another guest. Quickly he slipped the urn inside his jacket.

"Looking for a place to hide the urn?" the guest asked.

"Why would I need that?" the thief asked.

"Don't think I don't know what you're up to," the guest said.

"I was simply strolling in here to . . . to . . . take in the view from the window," the thief said. To back up his statement, he moved past the other guest.

Standing at the window, he glanced out. "I imagine at night this is a great place to view the urn — I mean, Saturn," he said.

"Nice try. Now it's my turn for the urn," the guest threatened.

"Or else?" the thief asked.

"Or I'll strangle you with the Rope," the guest said, displaying the weapon.

The first guest turned over the urn to the guest with the Rope.

The guest with the Rope fled into the only remaining room.

"I have a yearn for the urn, too," a voice there said.

The guest with the Rope was attacked by the remaining guest with the remaining weapon.

Having obtained the urn at last, the remaining guest gloated, "It's mine! And it's worth exactly five hundred sixty-five thousand dollars!"

WHO STOLE THE GREEK URN?
IN WHAT ROOM? WITH WHAT WEAPON?

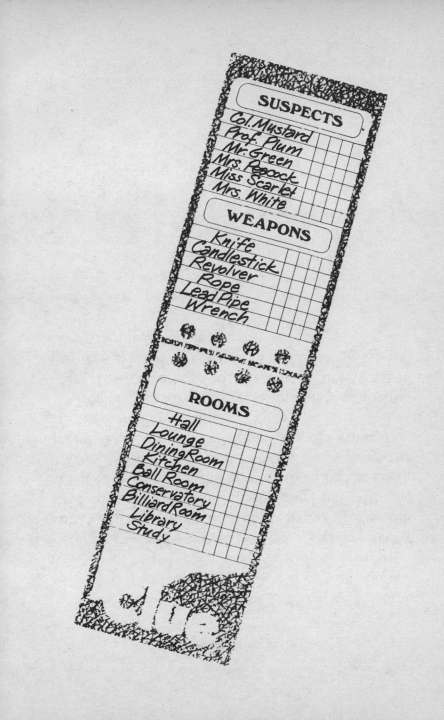

SOLUTION

MRS. PEACOCK in the CONSERVATORY with the KNIFE

Only two guests were present when Mr. Boddy disclosed the exact worth of the urn: Mrs. Peacock and Mrs. White. The female guest left with the task of cleaning up the flowers must be the maid, Mrs. White, which leaves Mrs. Peacock as the thief. The room and weapon were determined by process of elimination.

Luckily for Mr. Boddy, after a few moments, Mrs. Peacock was so offended by the nearly naked figures painted on the urn that she spurned it and returned it to him.

4.
Please Don't Sneeze

"**A**HH-CHOO!" SNEEZED MISS SCARLET so loudly that everyone else in the room jumped.

"Bless you, my dear," said Mr. Boddy. He was sitting in his favorite leather chair in the Library.

"Thank you," sniffled Miss Scarlet. "I'm afraid I'm getting a terrible cold."

"If you're cold," offered Professor Plum, "I'll be happy to make a fire."

"She's not cold," interrupted Mrs. White. "She's *getting* a cold. Which means she'll be filling this place with her nasty, infectious germs."

"Oh, how rude," said Mrs. Peacock. "I just hate germs. They're not polite."

"Yes," agreed Mr. Green, moving as far from Miss Scarlet as possible. "Don't breathe on me. I have important business to attend to next week and I can't afford to be sick."

"What nonsense," said Colonel Mustard. "We all know you can afford whatever you want."

"But not a cold," said Mr. Green, covering his nose and mouth with a handkerchief. "I think Miss

Scarlet should go home so she won't give her cold away."

"Miss Scarlet never gave anything away in her life," sneered Mrs. White.

"Take that back!" warned Miss Scarlet. "Or I'll sneeze on you."

"Maybe it's not just a cold," said Mrs. White. "Maybe you have the flu."

"*Flew*?" asked Professor Plum. "What *flew*? Don't tell me there's a bird loose somewhere in the mansion!"

"Go back to your reading," suggested Colonel Mustard, "before I challenge you to a duel."

"Ahh . . . ahh . . . ahh-chooo!" sneezed Miss Scarlet.

The other guests ducked for cover.

"Do you mind?" asked an angry Mrs. Peacock.

"Please excuse me," said Miss Scarlet, wiping her nose with a hankie.

"You should take that cold to some other room," said Mrs. Peacock.

"Maybe *you* should leave, instead," Miss Scarlet shot back.

"Please, everyone, let's not fight," said Mr. Boddy, closing his book. He got to his feet and went over to his huge antique desk.

He rummaged around in the drawers, mumbling to himself, "Now where did I leave that thing?"

"I hope he's looking for the Revolver, to take

care of that annoying Miss Scarlet," whispered Mr. Green.

"Better yet, maybe Mr. Boddy will find the Rope and strangle the next person who sneezes," said Mrs. White.

Mrs. Peacock covered her own nose and mouth with a prim lace hankie. "Oh, no," she moaned. "It seems I'm getting a bit of a cold myself."

"You mean you're under the weather?" asked Colonel Mustard.

Professor Plum thought for a moment, then said, "Aren't we all always under the weather?" he asked. "I mean, we're down here, the clouds are up there, and — " A sneeze interrupted him. "Oh, my goodness," he said. "My nose is starting to run."

"Then you'd best catch it," joked Mrs. White, before she, too, sneezed. "Maybe I'm allergic to something," she said.

"Like work?" asked Mrs. Peacock.

"Like you other guests," said Mrs. White.

"Well, real men are never bothered by a silly little cold," said Colonel Mustard. Then he sneezed. "Clear the way," he said. "I have to sit down!"

"You're worried about a 'silly little cold'?" mocked Miss Scarlet.

"Which I wouldn't have gotten if not for you!" stormed Colonel Mustard.

"Ah!" said Mr. Boddy, lifting a small brown

bottle from the drawer. "This should do the trick."

"Tricks are rude," said Mrs. Peacock.

"No," explains Mr. Boddy. "This isn't that sort of trick. It's my grandmother's secret cold-remedy medicine."

"If it's secret, how can you know it?" asked Professor Plum.

"I meant that it's been in my family for generations."

"Then maybe it's time to throw it out," said Mrs. White.

"Ahhh-choo!" sneezed Colonel Mustard. "I, for one, am willing to try anything to beat this horrible cold."

The guests moved closer to examine the brown glass bottle with the cork stopper.

"It looks deadly," said Mr. Green.

"Well, you shouldn't judge a book by its cover," said Mrs. Peacock.

"Or a bottle by its contents," added Mrs. White.

"Wait till you smell it," said Mr. Boddy.

He removed the lid, and a strong odor filled the room.

"Ahh," sighed Mr. Boddy. "It reminds me of my dear granny."

"I'm not taking that stuff!" said Miss Scarlet, moving away. "It smells like fish oil mixed with paint thinner."

"It smells like rotten cherries," said Colonel Mustard.

"It smells like one of Mrs. White's unsuccessful gourmet dinners," said Professor Plum. "Which reminds me — when is dinner?"

Mrs. White gave Professor Plum a withering look.

"If you ask me," she said, "it smells so bad that all of you should just leave the mansion at once to avoid it. And avoid germs! Good-bye! Farewell! It's been nice. Don't forget to write. Let me show you the door."

"Not so fast," said Mr. Boddy. "If you leave, you'll miss the treasure hunt I'm planning for tomorrow."

"Treasure?" said all the guests at once.

"Treasure," Mr. Boddy assured them. "But first you have to line up for this medicine. I want all my guests to stay healthy."

"But that stuff looks like it could kill us," protested Mr. Green.

"Do not fear," said Mr. Boddy. "One teaspoonful of grandma's cold remedy and you'll all be fit as fiddles."

"How fit is a fiddle?" pondered Professor Plum. "How fit is a flute, for that matter?"

"Come, come!" said Mr. Boddy. "Who'll be first?"

"All right, fine. I will," said Miss Scarlet. "Anything to feel better."

"I admire your willingness," said Mr. Boddy.

"I'm willing to go on a treasure hunt," replied

Miss Scarlet. She stood up in front of Mr. Boddy.

"Next?" said Mr. Boddy. "Let's form a line. The quicker we do this, the quicker you'll hear the details of the treasure hunt."

"I'll be next," said a male guest. "Let's hurry."

"Why?" asked Mr. Boddy.

"Because I have a duel to fight," the male guest explained.

"Professor, will you be third in line?" asked Mr. Boddy.

"No, I will," said a female, cutting in front of Professor Plum.

"Be my guest." Professor Plum moved behind her.

The remaining guests reluctantly lined up as well.

But Mrs. Peacock clearly wasn't happy. "It's very impolite to ask a woman to stand at the very end of the line," she said.

"Then sit down," kidded Mr. Green.

"You know what I mean," said Mrs. Peacock.

"Well then, madam," said a gracious Professor Plum, "let me trade places with you."

The two guests traded places.

But then the third guest in line moved to the front, claiming, "I need to be first because I have a lot of cleaning to do."

"If she gets to move up, then I do, too," said another guest.

"Hey, no cutting in line," moaned Colonel Mustard.

After much complaining, pushing, and shoving, the second person in line ended up last.

A moment later, when Mr. Boddy's back was turned, the new second guest in line moved up to the very front.

The other guests remained where they were.

Then the last person in line attempted to move up, but was turned back.

"Let me in," said another guest.

"Back in line," ordered the guest in front.

"Stop!" said Mr. Boddy. "Don't anyone move, or we'll be at this all night!"

IN WHAT ORDER ARE THE GUESTS STANDING?

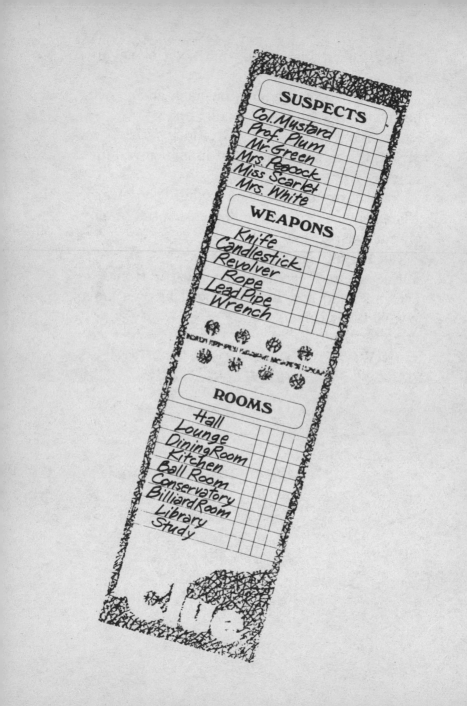

SOLUTION

COLONEL MUSTARD is first, MRS. WHITE is second, MRS. PEACOCK is third, MR. GREEN is fourth, PROFESSOR PLUM is fifth, and MISS SCARLET is last in line.

We started with Miss Scarlet first in line. We know the next guest was Colonel Mustard because he mentioned a duel. Following Mustard was a female guest who stepped in front of Professor Plum. Since Mrs. Peacock was last, the third guest was Mrs. White, followed by Professor Plum and Mr. Green.

To solve this mystery, one must only keep track of the guests as they switch positions.

Unfortunately (or fortunately), Mr. Boddy dropped the medicine bottle and broke it. It was a lucky break for the guests, who avoided the cold remedy altogether.

5.
For Goodness' Snakes!

"**A**HHHH!" SCREAMED MRS. WHITE AS she was dusting the Conservatory.

Colonel Mustard rushed in. "What's the matter?" he asked.

"There's a beast loose in the room!" said a shaken Mrs. White.

The colonel pulled the Wrench from his hunting jacket pocket. "Never fear, my good woman," he said. "I'll whack it a few times across the knees. That should teach it not to bother you ever again."

"But it doesn't have any knees," said Mrs. White.

"No knees?" asked Colonel Mustard.

"It doesn't have any legs, either," added Mrs. White.

While Colonel Mustard was mulling this over, Mrs. White pointed toward the floor.

"Ahhhhh!" she screamed again.

"Calm down," advised Colonel Mustard. "What exactly is it?"

She pulled the Revolver from her apron pocket.

"I thought I just saw an enormous snake," she said with a shudder.

"A snake?" asked Colonel Mustard. "Why would there be a snake of any size in the mansion?"

Before Mrs. White could offer an explanation, she saw something slither out of the room. "There it goes!" she yelled.

"After it!" shouted Colonel Mustard.

Mrs. White and Colonel Mustard followed it into the Ball Room. But instead of the snake, they found Miss Scarlet practicing ballet.

"Did you see a snake come in here?" asked Mrs. White.

"I haven't seen Mr. Green all day," said Miss Scarlet.

"I mean a real snake," said Mrs. White.

"No, I haven't," said an impatient Miss Scarlet. "And if you interrupt me again, I'll hit you with this," she added, picking up the Lead Pipe.

Suddenly, the gigantic snake appeared.

"There!" shouted Mrs. White.

"I hope it's not poisonous," said Miss Scarlet.

"If it's dead, it won't matter," said Colonel Mustard.

The three guests followed it into the Kitchen.

"Do you see it?" asked Mrs. White. "Oh, I hope it didn't get into my pots and pans!"

"I've heard that one can cook snakes," said Colonel Mustard.

"Not interested," said Mrs. White.

"Look!" shouted Miss Scarlet, pointing toward the door.

"Did you see the snake?" asked Colonel Mustard.

"If it wasn't a snake, it was a worm of frightening proportions," said Miss Scarlet.

The guests followed the snake into the Dining Room. There, Mrs. Peacock looked up from the table, where she was precisely positioning the Candlestick.

"Did you see a snake come in here?" demanded Colonel Mustard.

"How rude!" snapped Mrs. Peacock. "You need to ask in a polite manner."

Colonel Mustard took a deep breath. "Excuse me, but did you happen to see an amazingly large and potentially dangerous reptile of the snake variety make its way into this room?"

"No," said Mrs. Peacock.

"It's here somewhere," said Mrs. White, searching with her weapon at the ready.

"Don't be ridiculous," said Mrs. Peacock. "Everyone knows that the only snakes native to these parts are small and harmless garter snakes."

Miss Scarlet pointed toward the door. "Then explain that!"

The snake appeared, leaving the Dining Room.

Mrs. Peacock almost fainted. Then, after taking a moment to recover from the shock, she joined the others who had chased the snake into the Lounge.

As they rushed in, they encountered Mr. Green, who was reading the business section of the newspaper.

"What's so important that you storm in here?" he demanded.

"There's an enormously large and menacing snake loose in the mansion," reported Mrs. Peacock.

"Is there any way to make money with it?" asked Mr. Green, pulling out the Rope. "Perhaps we can use its skin to make some expensive cowboy boots."

"Well, here's your chance," said Colonel Mustard, seeing the snake leave the room and go into the Hall.

"Here," the colonel told Mrs. White. "Trade weapons with me and I'll hunt down the snake."

They all chased the snake into the Hall.

"For not having any legs," said Mr. Green, "that snake moves pretty darn fast!"

The group watched the snake slither right over Professor Plum's feet.

"Professor, watch out!" shouted Colonel Mustard.

"But I have my watch out already," said a puzzled Professor Plum, who never noticed the snake at all. He was standing beside the grandfather clock, using the Knife to adjust his pocket watch.

"Professor, sometimes you don't have a clue as to what's really going on," sighed Miss Scarlet.

"Thank you."

"Didn't you see the snake?" asked a winded Colonel Mustard.

Professor Plum chuckled. "A snake? Here in the mansion? Don't be ridiculous."

"What *are* you doing?" asked Miss Scarlet.

"I lost the stem to my watch," said Professor Plum, "and I'm trying to adjust the hands to the correct time."

"Meanwhile, an extraordinarily enormous snake just slid over your shoes," said Mrs. White.

"A snake? Are you sure?"

"Yes, a snake," said Mrs. Peacock. "A snake, like an adder."

"When I taught math many years ago, I had a couple of good adders in my class," said Professor Plum.

"We're talking about a real snake," said Mr. Green. "It's loose in the mansion."

"A snake in the mansion?" asked Professor Plum. "There must be some mistake."

"There goes the mistake — I mean, snake!" said Mrs. Peacock, pointing toward the Study. They all went into that room.

"Trade weapons with me," Mr. Green told Professor Plum, "and I'll take care of that slithering serpent."

The two guests traded weapons.

The guests began to search the room when Mr. Boddy entered, carrying a long, wooden stick.

"Good," said Miss Scarlet. "Our host is ready to join in the hunt."

"Hunt? What hunt? All this screaming and yelling and tramping through the mansion — you interrupted my billiard game," he said. "What's going on here?"

"There's a vicious, violent viper in the mansion," reported Mr. Green, trading weapons with the guest with the Candlestick.

"A viper?" asked Mr. Boddy.

"Like a vinshield viper?" asked Professor Plum.

"It's not a viper," said Mrs. Peacock. "It's some other kind of snake."

"Perhaps a kind of moccasin," added Colonel Mustard.

"Wait a moment," said Professor Plum. "A moccasin? I thought we were looking for a snake, not some kind of shoe."

"A moccasin is another kind of snake," explained Mrs. Peacock. "There are also cobras, mambas, sidewinders, and rattlesnakes."

"When did you become such an expert on snakes?" asked Mr. Green.

"Obviously, you never met *Mr.* Peacock," sneered Miss Scarlet.

"How rude!" said Mrs. Peacock.

"Stop this craziness right now," commanded Mr. Boddy.

"You're not afraid of the snake?" asked Mrs. White.

"Why should I be?" asked Mr. Boddy. "It's only my pet boa, Bobo."

"You have a pet snake?" asked Mrs. Peacock.

"A fine specimen of a constrictor," Mr. Boddy assured his guests.

"A boa constrictor?" asked Mrs. White.

"A snake that strangles its prey by wrapping itself around it and squeezing it until it dies," explained Mr. Boddy.

"Lovely," said Mrs. Peacock, covering her mouth with her lace hankie.

"I won't sleep with that thing in the mansion," insisted Miss Scarlet. "What if it wrapped itself around me?"

"I didn't know that you appealed to snakes," joked Mr. Green.

"And I thought, Miss Scarlet, that you liked wearing boas," added Professor Plum.

"I like boas made of feathers, not scales," said Miss Scarlet.

Mr. Boddy got down to the floor. "Here, Bobo," he called. "Come to papa."

But instead of coming to its owner, the frightened snake rushed out of the room.

"You've frightened poor Bobo," said Mr. Boddy.

"Not as much as he frightened us," said Miss Scarlet.

"After him!" shouted Mr. Green.

46

The person with the Wrench traded weapons with Miss Scarlet as the guests pursued the snake.

"Please don't harm Bobo," pleaded Mr. Boddy.

Outside the room, the guest with the Candlestick traded weapons with Colonel Mustard.

"I don't care what Mr. Boddy says," said Colonel Mustard. "When I find that boa, it'll go."

Colonel Mustard headed back to the Hall.

Mrs. Peacock took her weapon into the Lounge. "Wait until I find that snake in the grass — or should I say, in the Lounge," she told herself.

Professor Plum searched first the Dining Room and then another room.

Mr. Green tried first the Billiard Room and then another room.

Miss Scarlet returned to the room where she had been practicing ballet.

Mrs. White went into the Kitchen.

"Aaaah!" screamed a guest in the only room not mentioned.

"Oh, no!" said Mr. Boddy rushing to the scene. "Someone has murdered poor Bobo!"

But instead, he found a guest in Bobo's constricting grasp.

"Help me," the guest moaned, dropping the Revolver.

"It looks like you're in a bit of a squeeze," said Mr. Boddy.

"Call off your pet!" pleaded the trapped guest.

"Bobo may not have any arms," said a pleased

Mr. Boddy, "but he's giving you a hug you'll long remember."

"Help me," the guest whispered.

Instead, Mr. Boddy pulled up a chair and watched.

WHO'S CAUGHT BY THE SNAKE?
IN WHICH ROOM?

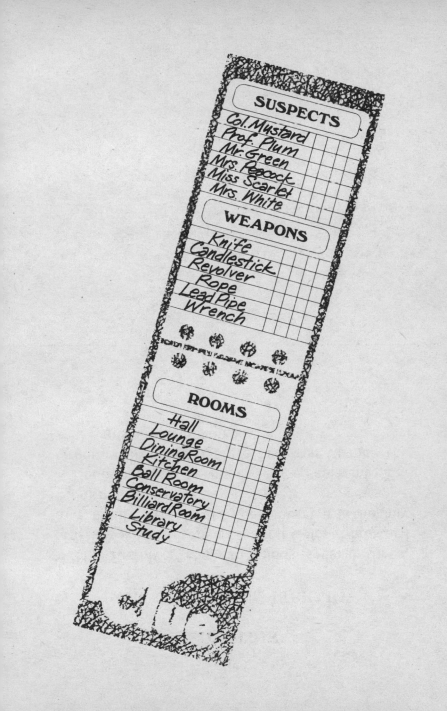

SOLUTION

MR. GREEN in the LIBRARY

The Revolver changed hands several times, starting with Mrs. White, then Colonel Mustard and, finally, Mr. Green. The Library was the only room not mentioned.

Bobo managed to squeeze some sense into Mr. Green, who never again considered turning the snake into a pair of cowboy boots.

6.
The Inky Trail

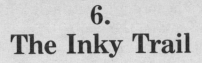

MR. BODDY HEADED TO THE STUDY TO do some very important paperwork. He quickly opened the safe and withdrew the documents he wanted, which he placed on the desk. He was in the room not more than a minute or two when he realized that he had left some files he needed upstairs.

Before leaving, he checked his gold pocket watch, which showed that it was two o'clock sharp.

He retrieved the files and returned to the Study at precisely 2:15 P.M. — and was shocked by what he found.

Someone had tried to forge his signature on a bond worth $250,000.

Luckily, the forger did not know that the fountain pen Mr. Boddy kept on that desk exploded when anyone other than its rightful owner used it.

Unluckily for Mr. Boddy, the exploding pen left a pool of ink that ruined the priceless Persian rug on the Study floor.

However, the forger unwittingly left a smudged handprint of ink on the wall.

"Wait until I get *my* hands on the forger," said an angry Mr. Boddy.

Going into the Hall, Mr. Boddy saw a second smudged handprint.

"I'll bet if I follow the inky trail of handprints, I'll find the guilty guest," he told himself.

Mr. Boddy peeked into the Lounge and saw a handprint there.

Next, he tried the Dining Room. He checked his watch. It was 2:20 P.M.

In the Dining Room, not only did Mr. Boddy see another smudged handprint, but he saw Professor Plum seated at the table. The professor was calmly snacking on some plums.

"Professor, I need a word with you," said Mr. Boddy.

"Of course," said Professor Plum. "Take several words with me, if you wish. Care for a plum?"

"No, thank you. Professor, were you in the Study recently?" asked Mr. Boddy.

"As a matter of fact, I was," said Professor Plum. "Ten minutes ago I thought I heard a commotion and went in there, but saw nothing suspicious."

"Your hands are stained," observed Mr. Boddy.

"From eating plums," said Professor Plum.

"Anything else you wish to tell me?" asked Mr. Boddy.

Professor Plum thought for a moment, then said, "These are very delicious plums."

Boddy excused himself and picked up the inky trail outside of the Dining Room. He followed it into the Kitchen, where he found Mrs. White busy at the sink.

"A moment of your time, please," said Mr. Boddy.

She turned around. "Yes, Mr. Boddy, may I help you?" she asked.

Noticing that her hands were stained with ink, Boddy thought that he'd found the forger. He checked his watch, which read 2:25.

"How could you?" he asked sadly.

"How could I what?" she replied.

"How could you go into the Study and use my pen to forge my name to a bond?" he asked.

"Sir, it's true I went into the Study," she admitted, "but only to check on Colonel Mustard."

"And when was that?"

She glanced at the oven clock. "Forty minutes ago," she said.

"I see," said Mr. Boddy.

"What's this about?" asked Mrs. White.

"Someone made a terrible mess in the Study while trying to take something from me," Mr. Boddy reported.

Mrs. White groaned, "Don't tell me someone tried to use your special pen and it exploded."

"I'm afraid so," said Mr. Boddy.

"Of course it's left to me to clean up the mess," noted Mrs. White. "I imagine it got all over that nice rug in there."

"Quite," said Mr. Boddy.

"Just what I need — more work," sighed Mrs. White.

"Mrs. White, I'm curious how you guessed so easily what happened," said Mr. Boddy.

"Having worked here at the mansion for years, I know all about your exploding fountain pen," said Mrs. White. "And certainly I know never to attempt to use it."

"Then why are your hands all inky?" asked Mr. Boddy.

"From preparing a seafood dinner with squid," she said, showing him the animal in the sink. "As you know, squids have ink sacs, which are an awful mess to clean," she added. "It looks like this is my day to deal with inky messes."

"I appreciate all the trouble you're going to," said Mr. Boddy. "But I'm still not convinced of your innocence."

"Talk about gratitude!" protested Mrs. White. "When I went to the Study, I used the secret passage connecting it with the Kitchen."

"Did anyone see you?" asked Mr. Boddy.

Mrs. White replied, "Colonel Mustard can attest to that, too."

"So?" said Boddy.

"Go ahead and look in the secret passage," she said. "See if you see any handprints."

Boddy did, and found no smudged handprints.

"It looks like I owe you an apology," he said.

"What you owe me is a big, fat raise!" said Mrs. White.

"Where is the colonel?" asked Mr. Boddy.

"Try the Conservatory, where he's conserving strength for his next duel," said Mrs. White.

Outside the Kitchen, Mr. Boddy picked up the inky trail of handprints leading in and out of the Ball Room. From there it went into the Conservatory, where Mr. Boddy expected to find Colonel Mustard.

Mr. Boddy did not find Colonel Mustard in the Conservatory. But he did find him — and Miss Scarlet — in the Billiard Room.

Entering, Mr. Boddy looked at his watch. It was 2:35.

"That's five straight games you've lost to me," Miss Scarlet was saying to Colonel Mustard. "Ready to quit?"

"Never!" stormed Colonel Mustard.

The two guests noticed Mr. Boddy.

"Oh, hello," Colonel Mustard said.

"An audience," cooed Miss Scarlet. "How lovely."

"I need a word with the colonel," explained Mr. Boddy.

"And he needs a few billiard lessons," said Miss Scarlet.

55

"Miss Scarlet, you're outrageous," said Colonel Mustard.

"I hope your aim with dueling pistols is better than your aim with a billiard cue," she said.

"Why don't we get out the pistols and find out?" said Colonel Mustard.

"Colonel," interrupted Mr. Boddy, "Mrs. White said she used the secret passage to the Study a little while ago to see if you needed anything."

"True, sir," said Colonel Mustard.

"And she said that you might be in the Conservatory," Mr. Boddy added.

"I was planning to go there," Colonel Mustard said, "until I was lured here by that pool hustler." He pointed to Miss Scarlet. As he spoke, he held up his hands, which were darkly stained.

"Colonel Mustard, you're not only a poor billiards player, you're a forger, too!" accused Mr. Boddy.

"Take back that insult this instant — or I'll challenge you to a duel!" shouted Colonel Mustard.

"Colonel, don't choose to duel with billiard sticks or you might lose," joked Miss Scarlet.

"How did you stain your hands?" asked Boddy.

"One of my dueling pistols accidentally fired when I was cleaning it," said Colonel Mustard. "Luckily, the only damage was these powder burns left on my hands."

"So you didn't go into the Study and forge my name to a bond?" asked Mr. Boddy.

"No, sir," said Colonel Mustard. "I went in there looking for some first aid cream. If you don't believe me, ask Miss Scarlet, who's been with me for the past hour."

"It hasn't been an hour," said Miss Scarlet. "It's been more like forty-five minutes since you accepted my challenge at billiards. Which means it's taken me an average of only nine minutes per game to beat you five games to none."

"Being a gentleman, I spotted you a few games," lied Colonel Mustard. "Let's play the first to win ten games and see how well you fare!"

"Given the average, we should be done in another forty-five minutes," said Miss Scarlet, hiding her hands behind her back.

"Why are you hiding your hands?" asked Mr. Boddy.

"Because I'm embarrassed by the terrible color nail polish I let Mrs. Peacock convince me to try in the Study," said Miss Scarlet, holding up her peacock blue-colored nails.

"Perhaps you're the forger," accused Mr. Boddy.

"You ask Mrs. Peacock," suggested Miss Scarlet.

"And where might I find her?" asked Mr. Boddy.

"I believe she's in the Lounge," said Miss Scarlet, "awaiting the start of *The Manners Hour* on the radio."

Mr. Boddy left the Billiard Room and went to the Library, but he found no handprint in that room.

From the Library, he went into the Lounge. There, he found Mrs. Peacock with her hands hidden under a pillow. She was listening to the radio.

Mr. Boddy glanced down at his watch, which read 2:47.

"Pardon me, Mrs. Peacock," he said.

"Yes?"

"Miss Scarlet claims that you and she were together in the Study, doing her nails," said Mr. Boddy.

"That's the truth," said Mrs. Peacock.

"And when was that?" asked Mr. Boddy.

"Let's see . . ." thought Mrs. Peacock aloud. "Lunch was over at one P.M., so it was no more than a half hour after that."

"And when did you leave the Study?" asked Mr. Boddy.

"I left when Miss Scarlet and Colonel Mustard began to discuss billiards. It's a game that I believe should not be brought up in decent company," said Mrs. Peacock.

Thinking he had found the forger, Mr. Boddy asked, "What's wrong with your hands?"

"I happened to spill something on them in the Study," admitted Mrs. Peacock.

"Nail polish?" asked Mr. Boddy.

"No, not nail polish," said an embarrassed Mrs. Peacock.

"Madam, let me see your hands," insisted Mr. Boddy.

She showed him her hands, which were stained.

"*You* are the forger!" accused Mr. Boddy.

"How rude!" said Mrs. Peacock.

"Then let's hear your explanation," demanded Mr. Boddy.

"After I left the Study, I went to my room and stayed there."

"You stayed there until . . . ?" asked Mr. Boddy.

"Until Mr. Green politely knocked on my door and asked if I wished to join him in painting some pictures," she said.

"Where?"

"Back in the Study," reported Mrs. Peacock.

"Ah!" said Mr. Boddy. "So you returned to the Study!"

"Only at Mr. Green's request," said Mrs. Peacock.

"And when was this?"

Mrs. Peacock consulted the small watch set in a cameo pin attached to her blouse. "I'd say thirty minutes ago."

"Go on," said Mr. Boddy.

"While with Mr. Green, I spilled some paint on my hands," Mrs. Peacock said. "To my horror, I wasn't able to wash all of it off. Being a lady, I did the only proper thing, which was to keep my hands hidden in public."

"And you expect me to believe this?" asked Mr. Boddy.

"Ask Mr. Green yourself," she said. "And, if you consider yourself any kind of a gentleman, you'll stay and join me for *The Manners Hour*, which comes on in just a few minutes."

Mr. Boddy listened to the first part of the radio show, then politely excused himself. He returned to the Study at precisely 3:15 P.M.

There he found Mr. Green putting away an easel and paints.

"Mrs. Peacock told me the two of you were painting together," said Mr. Boddy.

"That's true," said Mr. Green, holding up a painting. "Do you like it? I call it *Still Life with Fruit and Money*."

Mr. Boddy noticed that Mr. Green was trying to keep his hands hidden behind the painting.

"Is something wrong with your hands?" asked Mr. Boddy.

"Oh, you caught me," said Mr. Green with a guilty grin.

He took a rag and tried to wipe a stain from his hands.

"What is your explanation?" asked a suspicious Mr. Boddy.

"I stained my hands cleaning the brushes," reported Mr. Green.

"You were here in the Study?" asked Mr. Boddy.

"For just under an hour," said Mr. Green.

"Can anyone attest to your story?" asked Mr. Boddy.

"Ask my painting partner," said Mr. Green. "We came in here together."

Mr. Boddy did so at 3:20 P.M., and the guest backed up Mr. Green's claim.

"Thank you," said Mr. Boddy. "You helped me solve this mystery."

WHO IS THE FORGER?

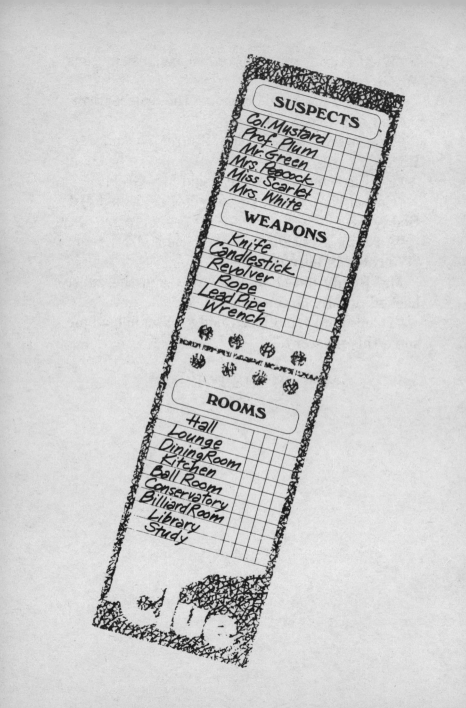

SOLUTION

PROFESSOR PLUM

There was only one guest who admitted to being in the Study between 2:00 and 2:15, when the crime took place.

Not only did Mr. Boddy make Professor Plum clean up the inky trail, but worse yet, he made him take over cleaning the squid.

7.
The Scavenger Hunt

IT WAS QUITE LATE ONE SATURDAY night and Mr. Boddy's guests were restless. But they were not tired, and it looked like they might stay up for hours.

"What are we going to do?" asked a bored Miss Scarlet.

"We could play charades," suggested Professor Plum.

"I'm not interested in a silly game like charades," said Mr. Green. "Now, if anyone wants to play a game that involves large sums of money, I'd be very interested."

"Is money the only thing you're interested in?" asked Mrs. White.

"Yes," replied Mr. Green without a second thought.

"I checked the TV listings earlier," reported Mrs. Peacock. "And there's an exciting program about to start on The Manners Channel. It's all about the proper use of the salad fork."

"I'll pass on the salad fork," said Professor Plum.

"If anyone is interested, I'd be happy to get out my scrapbook," offered Colonel Mustard. "It contains records of my favorite duels."

No one was interested.

"Well, if you're truly bored, you can help me clean up the Kitchen," suggested Mrs. White.

None of the guests were that bored.

"I say we drive into town and see a movie," said Miss Scarlet.

For a moment, this seemed like a winning idea.

"There's that new science fiction flick playing," said an eager Professor Plum.

"No thanks," sneered Mrs. Peacock. "I'd prefer a screen adaptation of one of the great classics of literature. Like *The Count of Monte Cristo*."

"*Count* me out," said Colonel Mustard. "But there is a war movie playing. Nothing like seeing a bit of blood and guts before bed."

Mrs. White waved a white handkerchief. "Not for me," she said. "I'm interested in seeing the one about the admirable working woman trapped in the mansion with a bunch of crazy guests."

"Hmmmm," said Professor Plum. "If my memory serves, I think I've seen that one."

"There's a love story starring two of Hollywood's romantic leads," suggested Miss Scarlet.

"Maybe we should just stay here," concluded Colonel Mustard.

"And do what?" snapped Miss Scarlet.

To avoid any more arguments over what to do,

Mr. Boddy came up with a plan. "Let's have a scavenger hunt!" he said.

"A what?" asked Mr. Green, who was counting all the change in his pocket.

"A scavenger hunt," repeated Mr. Boddy.

"How on earth do we hunt a scavenger?" asked Professor Plum.

"It's sort of a game," explained Mr. Boddy. "I give you a list of weapons to find around the mansion, and the person who finds the most weapons wins a prize."

"That doesn't sound like fun," complained Mrs. White. "All I *do* is pick up weapons around this mansion and put them back where they belong!"

"Well, I'd be interested in any kind of hunt," said Colonel Mustard.

"And I'd be interested in any sort of prize," added Miss Scarlet.

"I might be interested, depending on the prize," said Mrs. Peacock.

"It certainly is better than sitting around," offered Mr. Green. "Especially if the prize is money."

"Come on, Mr. Boddy," said Professor Plum. "Out with the prize."

"Hmm," thought Mr. Boddy aloud. "Let's see . . . Oh, I know! The winner gets to use my private yacht for a cruise to the Caribbean Islands."

"Oooh," said Miss Scarlet, doing a little rumba. "I can smell that tropical breeze right now."

"All I smell is your perfume," said Mrs. Peacock. "It's very rude for a lady to wear more than just a *dab* of perfume."

"A week on an island would do me a world of good," said Colonel Mustard. "It would give me time to clear my head."

"It would take more than a week to clear *his* head," said Mrs. White.

"A free trip to check my bank accounts in the islands?" mused Mr. Green.

"Come, come," said Mr. Boddy. "A scavenger hunt will be jolly fun."

"Count me in," said Mr. Green.

"Me, too," said Professor Plum.

"And me," added Mrs. Peacock.

"Oh, why not?" Mrs. White gave in.

"Good!" said Mr. Boddy. "Now, here's the list of weapons you must find," he explained, handing a piece of paper to each guest. "The Knife, the Lead Pipe, the Rope, the Revolver, the Candlestick, and the Wrench."

"But, being the maid, Mrs. White already knows where all those things are," protested Mrs. Peacock.

Mr. Green agreed. "Mrs. White has an unfair advantage."

"True," said Mr. Boddy. "Tell you what. I'll

take those six weapons and hide them myself. You all wait here in the Library until I'm done."

Ten minutes later . . .

Ten minutes later, Mr. Boddy returned.

"I've hidden the weapons," he announced.

"Where?" asked Professor Plum.

"It would make for a short game if I told," said Mr. Boddy.

"I don't need any hints. I will win easily without them. Let's get started!" demanded Colonel Mustard.

"Very well," said Mr. Boddy. "I will remain right here. In fifteen minutes I will ring a bell signaling the end of the hunt. We will gather here and find out who the winner is. Any questions?"

"Yes," said Professor Plum, raising his hand. "Tell me again why you can't say where you hid the weapons?"

"Ready, set, go!" said Mr. Boddy, ignoring the professor.

The guests pushed and shoved their way out of the room.

Once outside of the Library, they broke off and went their separate ways.

Professor Plum was first to reach the Conservatory. After a few moments, he located the Revolver.

After tearing through the Kitchen and finding

nothing, Mr. Green tried the Dining Room. There he was rewarded by the discovery of a weapon.

"If I were Mr. Boddy, where would I hide a weapon?" Colonel Mustard asked himself. After a moment's thought, he snapped his fingers. "I know."

He raced to the Billiard Room, but had no luck.

Taking her time, Mrs. Peacock found the Rope in the room where Mr. Green had found nothing.

Miss Scarlet calmly applied her lipstick. She wasn't worried because other guests had already found weapons. "That's why cheating was invented," she told herself.

She went into the Ball Room and saw Mrs. White picking up the Knife.

Miss Scarlet quickly hid behind the door and tackled Mrs. White as she attempted to leave.

Taken by surprise, Mrs. White dropped her weapon. Miss Scarlet picked it up and fled to the Kitchen.

Meanwhile, Colonel Mustard went to the Lounge, where he finally found a weapon — the Candlestick.

Lurking in the Kitchen, Miss Scarlet used the Knife to take the Wrench away from the guest who had found it in the Dining Room.

Everyone was now in pursuit of everyone else. Professor Plum chased a female guest into the Hall. Trapping her there, he ripped the weapon from her hands.

Hall. Trapping her there, he ripped the weapon from her hands.

Mrs. White, furious at losing the Knife, followed Mr. Green into the Library. "Give me your weapon before I knock you silly," she threatened.

"Why, Mrs. White, this is a side of you I haven't seen before," he said.

"Give me your weapon or you won't see much of anything," she warned.

"But I don't have one," Mr. Green cowered.

"Prove it," she snapped.

He emptied his pockets and showed her there was nothing up his sleeves.

"Just my luck," Mrs. White sighed, turning for the door.

Then Colonel Mustard spotted the guest with the Rope and the Revolver. "Hold it right there," he ordered. But the guest ignored him.

Colonel Mustard gave chase and caught the guest from behind. "It'll take a better man than you to outrun me," said Colonel Mustard.

But without warning, the other guest hit him on the head with the Revolver.

They struggled over the weapons and, in the process, the Rope shredded apart.

During this, a guest with no weapon arrived on the scene and sneaked off with the Revolver.

Just before Mr. Boddy was about to ring the bell signaling the end of the scavenger hunt, the guest with two weapons found the final weapon in the only room not previously mentioned.

WHO FOUND THE FINAL WEAPON?
IN WHAT ROOM?

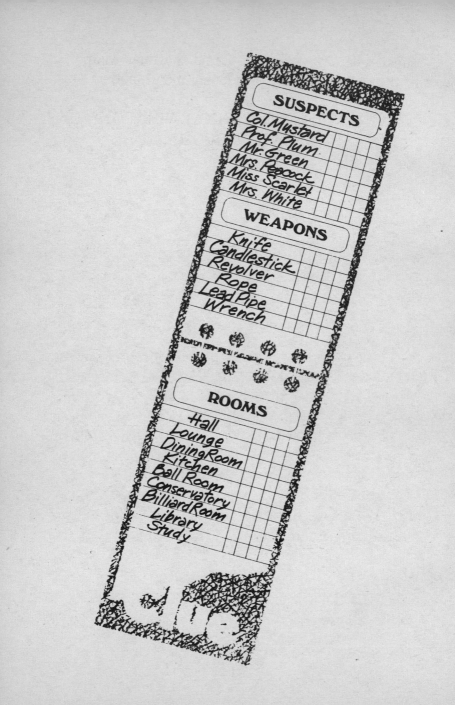

SOLUTION

MISS SCARLET found the **LEAD PIPE** in the STUDY.

By keeping track of the weapons, we know that Miss Scarlet ended up with the Knife and the Wrench. Either Mrs. Peacock, Mrs. White, or Mr. Green made off with the Revolver, leaving Colonel Mustard with the Candlestick and Professor Plum with the (shredded) Rope.

Miss Scarlet found the Lead Pipe in the only room not previously mentioned — the Study. However, because she cheated, the other guests went on the cruise in Miss Scarlet's place.

8.
Screaming for Ice Cream

THE GUESTS WERE VERY EXCITED BE-cause it was time for Mr. Boddy's monthly ice-cream tasting party. He and Mrs. White had worked for hours to make many different flavors of home-made ice cream from an old Boddy family recipe. The recipe called for the freshest milk and eggs. Furthermore, Mr. Boddy insisted that only the finest flavors, gathered from around the world, be used. Needless to say, no expense was spared.

After testing each flavor and making any nec-essary adjustments to the recipe, Mr. Boddy said, "I believe we have the most delicious ice cream in the world."

"I hope so," said Mrs. White, wiping her brow.

Mr. Boddy gathered his guests and an ex-hausted Mrs. White in the Kitchen.

"I have a *scoop* for you. The ice cream is ready!" he exclaimed.

"Hooray, hooray! Hooray for ice cream!" yelled Professor Plum.

"He's such a dip," muttered Mrs. White.

"A *double dip*," agreed Mr. Green, who overheard the comment.

"A dip who drips," added Miss Scarlet.

"But as a friend, I can't be *licked*," said Professor Plum, coming to his own defense.

"But we can't eat ice cream today," said Mr. Green.

"And why not?" asked Mrs. Peacock.

"Because it's not a *sundae!*" he joked.

Mrs. Peacock rolled her eyes. "With all of your money," she told Mr. Green, "you could afford to find someone to write you better jokes."

"You're all a bunch of *cone*heads," observed Colonel Mustard.

"Take that back before someone pours hot fudge over you," warned Miss Scarlet.

"Ahem," interrupted Mr. Boddy. "Shall we begin our tasting party? We have to select the flavor of the month."

"Just a moment," said Mrs. Peacock. "I must remind all of you that I cannot eat nuts of any kind, so please don't serve me anything with nuts."

"She's *nuts* herself," sneered Mrs. White.

"And I don't eat fruit," reminded Mr. Green.

"He is so *bananas*," whispered Mrs. White.

"And I only want the low-fat flavors," requested Miss Scarlet. "I try to watch my calories."

"How does one *watch* calories?" mused Professor Plum, putting on his glasses. "Well, all the flavors look good enough to eat," he concluded.

"Let's begin," said Mr. Boddy, tapping his silver spoon on his glass. "Please be seated."

The guests sat on stools at the Kitchen counter.

"Just one last thing," said Mrs. White. She went to a drawer and brought out six plastic bibs.

"Ah, do we have to wear bibs?" complained Colonel Mustard.

"I'm not cleaning up any more spills," said Mrs. White.

"But I won't spill — I promise!" whined Mr. Green.

"No bibs, no ice cream," said Mrs. White.

The guests each put on a bib.

"May we continue?" asked Mr. Boddy.

Satisfied, Mrs. White nodded.

Mr. Boddy explained, "There are six new flavors for you to try. Starting with this one."

He put the first bowl in the center of the counter.

"This first one I've named Chocolate Mustache," he said. "It is low fat, as is the last flavor we'll taste."

"But why is it called Chocolate Mustache?" asked Mrs. Peacock.

"Because you'll like it so much you'll have a chocolate mustache when you're done," replied Mr. Boddy.

"How rude!" said Mrs. Peacock. But she tasted it anyway.

Several of the other guests tried it as well, but not Professor Plum.

"I already have a mustache," he explained.

"So do I," said Colonel Mustard. "But that's not stopping me."

Mrs. White also declined. "I'm not playing this silly tasting game," she told the other guests.

After the guests finished with the first bowl, Mr. Boddy traded it for a second. "The next flavor is called Jalapeño Pepper," he said.

"Aren't jalapeños hot?" asked Mr. Green.

"Very," said Mr. Boddy.

"Hot ice cream?" asked Professor Plum. "You mean it's melted already?"

"Hot as in spicy," explained Mr. Boddy.

"Then I decline," said Mr. Green. "Hot food doesn't agree with me."

Mrs. White didn't try it, either. She sat next to a sulking Miss Scarlet and watched the other guests dig in.

Then Mr. Boddy brought out a third flavor with lumps of something pink in it. "What is this concoction?" asked Colonel Mustard.

"Bubble Gum Surprise," said Mr. Boddy.

"What's the surprise?" asked Professor Plum.

"Those lumps are pieces of gum. After you're finished eating the ice cream, you get to blow bubbles," said Mr. Boddy.

"Phooey!" muttered Miss Scarlet.

The other guests dug in, except for Professor Plum, and once done with the ice cream, blew large pink bubbles.

"Gum sticks to my teeth," the professor explained, "and I can't find my dental floss."

"Remind us to make Dental Floss flavor for the professor next time," chided Mrs. White, bypassing a taste herself.

"I'm still hungry," said Colonel Mustard. "What's next?"

"Now we will try my personal favorite," said Mr. Boddy. "It's a brand-new flavor called Hot Dog and Marshmallow."

"That sounds dreadful!" said Mrs. Peacock. "Whoever heard of putting hot dogs in ice cream?"

"It's great during the summer," said Mr. Boddy. "You can have all the flavors of a picnic without using the grill."

"It's actually not bad," said Mr. Green, taking the first bite, "although it could use a little mustard."

"I hope you're referring to the condiment and not to me," said Colonel Mustard.

The others, except for Miss Scarlet and the guests who didn't try the Bubble Gum and the Chocolate Mustache,tried this new flavor.

"What's left to try?" asked Professor Plum.

"A simple but delicious flavor, Peanut Butter," said Mr. Boddy, putting a dish of brown ice cream in the middle of the counter. "I know one of you doesn't eat nuts, but the others may enjoy it."

And they did.

"And for our final flavor of the month," Mr. Boddy concluded, "may I present Low-Fat Fruitcake. Perfect for the holidays."

The guests suspiciously eyed the strange-looking ice cream with bits of candied fruit and nuts.

"Well," said Miss Scarlet, "if it's low fat, I'll try it. It can't be worse than my cousin Rose's fruitcake. Each year she sends me one and I use it as a bookend until she sends me the next one."

"The best way to avoid any fat is to avoid tasting it at all," said Mrs. White, turning up her nose.

But everyone else, except for the guests who didn't like fruit or nuts, tried the exotic flavor.

"Makes me think of Christmas," said Professor Plum, rather tearfully. "Let's all sing 'Heck the Dolls'! I mean, 'Deck the Halls'!"

"It's rude to sing at the table," pointed out the always-proper Mrs. Peacock. "Besides, I'm too full to sing."

The others agreed.

"While you each decide your favorite flavor, I'd like to hear from the guest who tried them all," said Mr. Boddy.

WHO TRIED ALL SIX FLAVORS OF ICE CREAM?

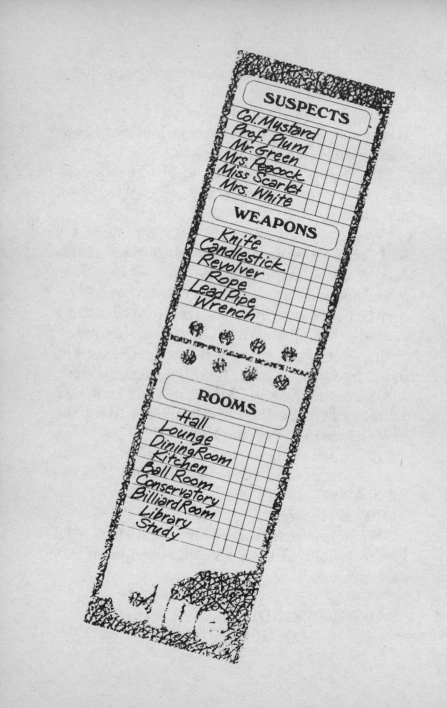

SOLUTION

COLONEL MUSTARD

Mrs. Peacock tried all but Peanut Butter and Fruitcake. Mr. Green tried four flavors, Professor Plum tried three, Miss Scarlet tried both low-fat kinds and Peanut Butter, and Mrs. White tried only Peanut Butter.

Surprisingly, the guests voted Hot Dog and Marshmallow as Flavor of the Month. In fact, they liked it so much they decided to have it for dinner — with pickles on the side.

9.
Caught Bare-handed

*C*RASH! BAM! SHATTER!

A thundering noise suddenly echoed through the mansion.

All of Mr. Boddy's guests stopped what they were doing and froze in place.

The next thing they heard was Mr. Boddy shouting. His voice echoed through the mansion.

"Thief! Thief! One of you is a thief!"

Although in separate rooms in the mansion, a few of the guests followed Mr. Boddy's voice and found him in the Dining Room.

"What's the matter?" asked Miss Scarlet.

"See for yourself," said Mr. Boddy.

He was standing sadly next to his priceless crystal chandelier, which had fallen and shattered on the floor.

"How did that happen?" Miss Scarlet asked, placing a white-gloved hand on his shoulder.

"You don't know?" asked Mr. Boddy.

"How would I know?" she said. "I was reading in the Study when I heard a terrible commotion."

"I'll tell you how it happened," said a red-faced

Mr. Boddy. "One of you attempted to steal my chandelier."

"How do you know it didn't just fall on its own?" asked Professor Plum.

"Where were you?" Mr. Boddy asked.

Professor Plum playfully punched Mr. Boddy in the arm with his boxing glove. "I was practicing my punches in the Ball Room."

"Yes, and I see you're as *punchy* as ever," commented Mrs. White, coming in from the Kitchen. She was wearing rubber gloves — the kind used for washing dishes.

"Mrs. White," said Miss Scarlet, "those rubber gloves are a lovely yellow, but I don't think they match your outfit very well."

"Mr. Boddy thinks someone tried to make off with his chandelier," Professor Plum told Mrs. White.

"I've witnessed some crazy things," she said, "but stealing a chandelier?"

"It's quite valuable, I assure you," said Mr. Boddy. "It once hung in the Palace of Versailles, where the French kings used to live."

"Oooo-la-la," said Miss Scarlet. "It must be worth a king's ransom."

"It *was*," sighed Mr. Boddy.

"Very well," said Mrs. White. "But what makes you so certain that it didn't simply fall on its own?"

"A-ha!" exclaimed Mr. Boddy. "I'll tell you how I know that the chandelier didn't fall." He directed his guests' attention toward the ceiling. "Look there at the cable that held the chandelier up. It's been cut clean through."

Sure enough, the guests could clearly see that the heavy cable had been severed.

"Where are the other guests?" asked Mr. Boddy.

"No doubt hiding the ladder needed to reach the ceiling," said Miss Scarlet.

"Mrs. White, please have everyone join us," instructed Mr. Boddy. "I'm going to dust this room for fingerprints."

"Well, at least someone besides me will do the dusting," she said.

Mrs. White left. After a few minutes Mrs. Peacock entered. "Mrs. White said you wished to see me."

"Where were you?" asked Mr. Boddy.

"I was in the Conservatory," she explained, "weeding the violets. Weeds are so very rude!" Mrs. Peacock clapped her hands together for emphasis, but the sound was muffled by her gardening gloves.

Meanwhile, Mr. Boddy was busy dusting the room for prints — including the walls, the chairs, and the dining room table.

"Yes!" he shouted. "Here it is! A full set of prints for the left hand."

Then Mr. Green entered. "Mrs. White demanded that I come here," he said.

"Where have you been?" asked Mr. Boddy, looking up.

Mr. Green stood sheepishly, his hands behind his back.

"Well?" asked Mr. Boddy.

Mr. Green stammered and mumbled. Finally, he showed everyone his hands. They were covered by short pink cotton gloves.

"Now those are very attractive," said Miss Scarlet. "Better than those yellow ones Mrs. White is wearing."

"Why are you wearing gloves?" snickered Professor Plum.

"Yes, it's very rude for a gentleman to wear gloves indoors," agreed Mrs. Peacock.

"If you must know," said Mr. Green in a low voice, "I was in the Lounge, giving myself a manicure."

"A manicure!" hooted Colonel Mustard, who had entered in time to hear this revelation. "Real men don't get manicures. Real men fight duels."

"I've found that if I keep my fingernails short, I have an easier time counting money," explained Mr. Green.

Colonel Mustard began to laugh, until Mr. Boddy's stare made him stop. "Where have you been?" asked Mr. Boddy, keeping his gaze directed at Colonel Mustard.

"I was in the Hall, practicing my fencing," said

Colonel Mustard. To demonstrate, he thrust his rapier at the guests with professional flair.

"Maybe he's the thief who tried to steal the chandelier," said Mrs. White, returning. "Look. He's only wearing one glove."

"I don't know what you're talking about, Mrs. White," huffed Colonel Mustard. "First of all, I have no interest in a bunch of little, shiny crystals, and second of all — fencers only wear *one glove!* And thirdly, my good woman, you'll notice that my other hand, my left hand, is completely bandaged." He showed his hand, which was tightly wound with white medical tape.

"What happened to you?" asked Professor Plum, very concerned.

"Just a little burn," said Colonel Mustard. "I was practicing my flamethrowing the other day and I had a near miss."

"You're lucky you didn't burn the mansion down," said Mrs. White.

"If you're finished, I'd like to return to my weeding," Mrs. Peacock told Mr. Boddy.

"Yes, yes," added Mr. Green, "get on with it."

Mr. Boddy concluded his fingerprinting and took out a chart of prints.

"What's that?" asked Mr. Green.

"I took the liberty of having the local police send me copies of everyone's fingerprints," said Mr. Boddy, "just in case."

"How rude!" said Mrs. Peacock.

"When did you do that?" asked Miss Scarlet.

"Last year, after I invited you all for the weekend and later found all of my silverware missing," explained Mr. Boddy.

"Oh, that," said a blushing Professor Plum.

"That was then, this is now," said Colonel Mustard. "Who do you think tried to steal the chandelier?"

"I'll tell you in a moment," said Mr. Boddy.

"Well," said Mrs. White, looking around. "It couldn't have been any of us. We're all wearing gloves. You can't leave a fingerprint if you're wearing gloves."

Mr. Boddy smiled and looked around. "Sadly, my dear guests, the thief is among us. And the thief *was* wearing a glove."

"It must be Colonel Mustard," said Mrs. Peacock. "He could have put that tape on his hand after he cut the cord."

"No," said Mr. Boddy. "It was not Colonel Mustard.

WHO WAS THE THIEF?

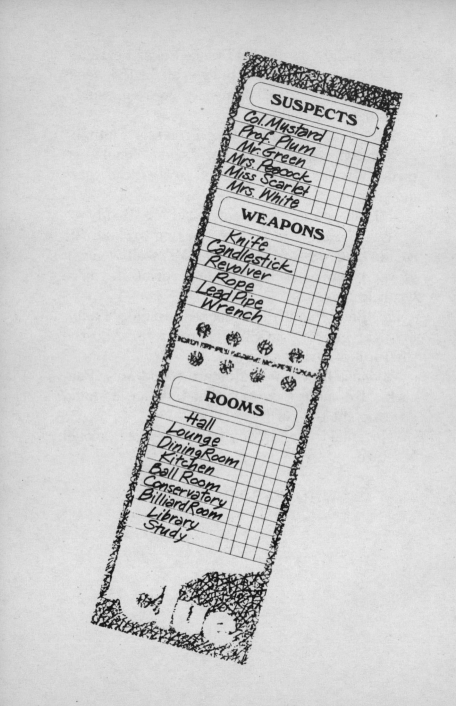

SUSPECTS

Col. Mustard				
Prof. Plum				
Mr. Green				
Mrs. Peacock				
Miss Scarlet				
Mrs. White				

WEAPONS

Knife				
Candlestick				
Revolver				
Rope				
Lead Pipe				
Wrench				

ROOMS

Hall				
Lounge				
Dining Room				
Kitchen				
Ball Room				
Conservatory				
Billiard Room				
Library				
Study				

SOLUTION

MISS SCARLET

Mr. Boddy told the guests that the thief wore *a glove*. We know that the thief isn't Colonel Mustard, and Miss Scarlet is the only guest who isn't described as wearing gloves on both hands. Poor Miss Scarlet had to put on Mrs. White's yellow rubber gloves and wash dishes until she earned enough money to repair the chandelier.

10.
Revenge of the Mummy

ON THEIR LAST NIGHT IN THE MAN-
sion, Mr. Boddy called his guests into the Ball
Room. He was standing on the stage, beside a
large object draped by a sheet. Knowing that Mr.
Boddy always saved a surprise for the last night,
the guests were abuzz trying to guess what it was.

"Perhaps he has a stack of gold bars under the
sheet," said a hopeful Mr. Green.

"Or a sculpture of himself," suggested Mrs.
White.

"What's the mystery?" asked Colonel Mustard.

"Please, the suspense is killing me," said Miss
Scarlet, covering a yawn.

Finally, Mr. Boddy removed the sheet, expos-
ing an old, wooden, elongated box painted with
strange symbols. It was wrapped in a heavy chain,
which was held shut by a large lock.

"Where'd you dig that thing up?" joked Miss
Scarlet.

"Kicking around yard sales?" kidded Professor
Plum.

"Say what you wish," said Mr. Boddy. "In fact, this is a very valuable item."

"That thing?" asked Mrs. White.

" 'That *thing*' is the coffin of an ancient pharaoh, which I recently acquired during a trip to Egypt," explained Mr. Boddy.

"You mean there's a mummy inside there?" asked Mr. Green.

"There's a *mommy* trapped inside?" said an alarmed Professor Plum. "Quick, let her out!"

"A mummy, not a mommy," said Mr. Boddy.

"A dried-up dead body wrapped in cloth?" asked Mrs. White. "Don't ask *me* to change those sheets!"

"Wasn't it the custom to bury the pharaohs with all of their treasures?" asked Mrs. Peacock.

"Quite correct," said Mr. Boddy.

"So there must be a fortune in gold and jewels inside this box?" asked Colonel Mustard.

"Perhaps," answered Mr. Boddy.

The guests began to elbow and push their way toward the coffin.

"But I must warn you," said Mr. Boddy, stopping them. "The curse of the mummy's revenge also comes with this coffin. Whoever takes the treasure shall be cursed!"

"I'd dig up the desert for the chance to look at the treasure," mused Miss Scarlet.

"There's no denial — I want the riches of the Nile," said Mr. Green.

"Curses are silly things," said a dismissive Colonel Mustard.

The intrigued guests immediately began plotting to raid the mummy's coffin.

"Now, I must ask you all to leave the room," insisted Mr. Boddy.

"Why?" asked Professor Plum.

"Because I don't want anyone to risk the mummy's revenge," he said.

The guests reluctantly did as Mr. Boddy asked, even as their minds were busy plotting.

Assured that the guests had gone upstairs, Mr. Boddy turned out the lights. On his way out, he closed the door behind him.

Several hours later . . .

Several hours later, a male guest entered the darkened Ball Room carrying the Lead Pipe.

He took several swipes at the lock holding the chain around the wooden coffin, but was unable to knock it loose.

"Here, let me give it a whack," said a female, entering with the Wrench.

But she, too, was unable to free the lock.

Then another male guest entered, carrying the Candlestick.

"Perhaps I can *shed some light* on the matter," he said.

"Oh, Professor Plum, you're just the man we need," said the female.

Yet, even with the added light, the three of them couldn't budge the lock.

Then a second female entered with the Rope. "I say we tie one end around the lock," she said, "and try to yank it off."

However, in trying to tie the rope around the lock, she broke a red-polished fingernail.

"Oh, no!" she moaned. "This is horrible!"

"That we can't budge the lock?" asked Professor Plum.

"No, that I broke a nail," said Miss Scarlet.

"Never fear," said a third male guest, entering with the Knife. "I'll bet I can pick the lock."

But he couldn't.

The last guest entered, carrying the Revolver.

"Stand clear," the guest ordered, "and I'll blast the lock off!"

Before the guest could pull the trigger, Mr. Boddy entered and turned on the light.

"A-ha!" he exclaimed. "I figured you'd try to steal my mummy."

The guests apologized and started to head for their bedrooms, when Mr. Boddy stopped them.

"Don't you want to see what's inside?" he asked. "I must say, my own curiosity has gotten the best of me."

The guests eagerly returned.

Mr. Boddy took out a key and opened the lock.

The guests peered inside the wooden coffin. It was empty.

"Now see what you've done!" said Mr. Boddy. "The mummy came to life and escaped before you could plunder the treasure!"

But no one believed Mr. Boddy.

"Mr. Boddy, you tricked us. There never was a mummy or a treasure," said Colonel Mustard, waving the Knife. "I should challenge you to a duel."

"Believe what you wish," said a coy Mr. Boddy. "But if you know what's good for you, you'll believe in the mummy's revenge."

"No treasure?" asked Mrs. Peacock, putting down the Revolver.

"At least not in this room," said Mr. Boddy.

"I want my mummy — I mean, mommy," moaned Miss Scarlet, still worried about her broken fingernail.

"Looks like I had the final laugh. You all might as well go to your rooms and get a good night's sleep," said Mr. Boddy.

The guests trudged off.

But immediately after leaving the room, they each started searching for the mummy and the treasure that they were convinced existed.

"I'll bet I know how to take the wraps off this mystery," said Mrs. Peacock. She headed for the only room which ended in an E, but found no mummy or treasure there.

After searching the Kitchen, the other two females exchanged weapons.

"The mummy is definitely not in any room that ends in Y," reported Colonel Mustard, momentarily joining the others.

"And it's not in the Billiard Room," added Mrs. Peacock.

The guests separated again and went their own ways.

Later, Professor Plum and Mr. Green ran into each other in the Hall, where neither of them could find the mummy.

Finally, a guest entered the remaining room, where a figure was seated in the dark.

"Don't bother trying to turn on the light," the figure said. "I've made this room as dark as my tomb."

"I've come to the right place," said the guest.

"Yes," the figure congratulated the guest. "But now you must learn about the curse of the mummy's revenge."

"Which is . . . ?" the skeptical guest asked.

The figure lit a candle.

The guest stood in horror, as the mummy itself was illuminated.

"So the curse is real!" moaned the guest.

"Worse yet, there never was a treasure," said the figure wrapped in strips of ancient cloth. "I fooled you, just as I fooled Mr. Boddy and every other fortune hunter!"

The guest took a closer look at the figure.

"Wait a moment," the guest said, "you're Mr. Boddy in disguise!"

The mummy laughed. "You're wrong," it said.

"No, I'm not!" shouted the furious guest, and used a weapon to strangle the figure the guest believed was Mr. Boddy.

WHO MURDERED MR. BODDY?

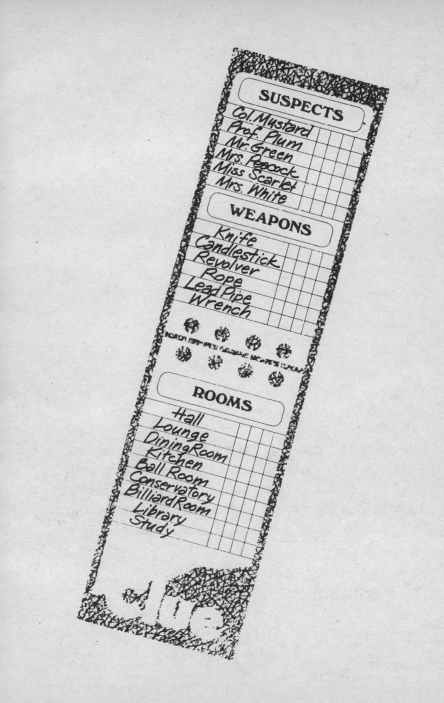

SOLUTION

MRS. WHITE in the DINING ROOM
with the ROPE

By process of elimination, we know where the murder took place. Because Boddy was strangled, we know that the murder weapon was the Rope. Miss Scarlet originally had the Rope, but she exchanged it for Mrs. White's Wrench.

Get a clue...
Your favorite board game is a mystery series!

by A.E. Parker

☐	BAM46110-9	#1	Who Killed Mr. Boddy?	$3.50
☐	BAM45631-8	#2	The *Secret* Secret Passage	$2.99
☐	BAM45632-6	#3	The Case of the Invisible Cat	$2.95
☐	BAM45633-4	#4	Mystery at the Masked Ball	$2.95
☐	BAM47804-4	#5	Midnight Phone Calls	$3.25
☐	BAM47805-2	#6	Booby Trapped	$3.50
☐	BAM48735-3	#7	The Picture Perfect Crime	$3.25
☐	BAM48934-8	#8	The Clue in the Shadow	$3.50
☐	BAM48935-6	#9	Mystery in the Moonlight	·$3.50
☐	BAM48936-4	#10	The Case of the Screaming Skeleton	$3.50
☐	BAM62374-5	#11	Death by Candlelight	$3.50
☐	BAM62375-3	#12	The Haunted Gargoyle	$3.50
☐	BAM62376-1	#13	The Revenge of the Mummy	$3.50
☐	BAM62377-X	#14	The Dangerous Diamond	$3.50
☐	BAM13742-5	#15	The Vanishing Vampire	$3.50
☐	BAM13743-3	#16	Danger After Dark	$3.99

Available wherever you buy books, or use this order form

Scholastic Inc., P.O. Box 7502, 2931 East McCarty Street, Jefferson City, MO 65102

Please send me the books I have checked above. I am enclosing $_____ (please add $2.00 to cover shipping and handling). Send check or money order—no cash or C.O.D.s please.

Name_____ Birthdate_____

Address_____

City_____ State/Zip_____

Please allow four to six weeks for delivery. Offer good in U.S. only. Sorry mail orders are not available to residents of Canada. Prices subject to change.   CL996